Lion dance

Banquet

Night market

Candied fruit

Pork belly bun

Chopsticks

Rice

Taipei 101

MRT (Mass Rapid Transit)

Red envelope

Mango

To all families with a loved one faraway —M. C. G.

To Jenya, Joline, and Elim
and to my wonderful family and pals with whom
I have eaten and adventured in Taiwan —T. S.

BLOOMSBURY CHILDREN'S BOOKS
Bloomsbury Publishing Inc., part of Bloomsbury Publishing Plc
1385 Broadway, New York, NY 10018

BLOOMSBURY, BLOOMSBURY CHILDREN'S BOOKS, and the Diana logo are trademarks of Bloomsbury Publishing Plc

First published in the United States of America in January 2022
by Bloomsbury Children's Books

Text copyright © 2022 by Margaret Chiu Greanias
Illustrations copyright © 2022 by Tracy Subisak

Bloomsbury books may be purchased for business or promotional use. For information on bulk purchases please contact
Macmillan Corporate and Premium Sales Department at specialmarkets@macmillan.com

Library of Congress Cataloging-in-Publication Data
available upon request
ISBN 978-1-5476-0721-1 (hardcover) • ISBN 978-1-5476-0873-7 (e-book) • ISBN 978-1-5476-0872-0 (e-PDF)

Art created with India ink, Japanese watercolor, pastel, and colored pencil on Fabriano Artistico watercolor paper
Typeset in Source Sans Pro Semibold
Book design by John Candell
Printed in India by Replika Press Pvt Ltd, Sonipat, Haryana
2 4 6 8 10 9 7 5 3 1

To find out more about our authors and books visit www.bloomsbury.com and sign up for our newsletters.

Amah Faraway

Margaret Chiu Greanias

illustrated by
Tracy Subisak

Have an adventure!
—MCGreanias

BLOOMSBURY
CHILDREN'S BOOKS

NEW YORK LONDON OXFORD NEW DELHI SYDNEY

It was time for a visit.
Kylie squirmed.

We can . . . eat yummy new foods.
We can . . . go to pretty new places.
We can . . . have an adventure!

And,
we get to see Amah.
It'll be *so fun*.

One hundred butterflies took flight in Kylie's belly.
Kylie and Amah didn't visit each other often enough.

Every Saturday,
they connected by computer.

Amah
told stories to
Kylie,

Amah
sang songs to
Kylie,

Amah
showed snacks to
Kylie,

always speaking simply and slowly.

But Kylie jittered and jiggled in her seat—
video chats *weren't* the same as real life.

Kylie held tight to
Mama.
With
ears pricked, she listened to Amah talk.
Kylie *kind* of understood.

In Amah's apartment, everything seemed strange.

Yet . . .

the faces were happily familiar.

Aunts, uncles, and cousins (actual . . . or not?) packed a banquet for Mama and Kylie.
Ten twelve-person tables
and over nine courses of steaming food!
GULP!

Kylie ate . . . rice.

Finally.

Amah treated them to the Chinese donuts, yóutiáo, she delighted in.

Hǎochī,
好吃
Yummy!

No frosting, no filling, no CHOCOLATE?

Amah brought them to
the parks
she enjoyed.

Kylie eyed Amah sideways.

Amah took them shopping
at the night market—where
she seemed to try and buy *everything*.

Everywhere they went,
Kylie
trailed behind
Amah and Mama.

It was a brand-new day,
the day they visited the hot springs.
Kylie changed.
After, she dipped a toe in the water.
Amah
beckoned.

Kylie loved splashing . . .
and
the water *was* warm.
Should
she?
Could
she?

She
could!
She
should!
The water was warm!
And
Kylie *loved* splashing.

Kylie
beckoned.

Amah!

After she dipped a toe in the water . . .
Kylie changed!
The day they visited the hot springs?
It was a brand-new day.

She delighted in
the Chinese donuts, yóutiáo,
Amah treated them to.

Finally,
Kylie ate rice . . .
GULP!
and over nine courses of steaming food!

Ten twelve-person tables—
aunts, uncles, and cousins (actual or not) packed a banquet for Mama and Kylie.
The faces were happily familiar.

Yet . . .

. . . in Amah's apartment, everything seemed strange.
Kylie kind of understood.
Ears pricked, she listened to Amah talk
with
Mama.

Kylie held tight to
Amah
when they arrived at the Taipei airport.

One lived in Taipei. One lived in San Francisco.
Video chats *weren't* the same as real life.
But Kylie jittered and jiggled in her seat.
Always speaking simply and slowly,

Kylie
showed snacks to
Amah,

Kylie
sang songs to
Amah,

Kylie
told stories to
Amah.

They connected—by computer—
every Saturday.

Kylie and Amah didn't visit each other often enough.
One hundred butterflies took flight in Kylie's belly.

It'll be *so fun*!
We get to see Amah,

and
we can have an adventure!
We can go to pretty new places!

We can eat yummy new foods!

Kylie squirmed.

It was time . . . for a visit.

A NOTE FROM THE AUTHOR

"Amah" is, as you may have understood from reading this book, the Taiwanese word for grandmother. Like Kylie, I lived in the United States while my amah lived in Taipei. We visited each other once every year or two. Since I was shy and we didn't see each other often, whenever I *did* see her, I always hung back a little in the beginning.

When she visited *us*, I would wait nearby as she unpacked, and peek at the goodies she had brought. I still remember the herbal smell that filled the room when she unzipped her suitcase. I would grow more comfortable with her as each day passed, until we were buddies. One time, as she was leaving my family in New York to visit my uncle's family in New Jersey, I didn't want her to leave, so I went with her!

A couple of times, *we* visited *her*. That was a bigger adjustment. Both she *and* Taipei felt unfamiliar to me. Not to mention that I only spoke a little bit of Taiwanese. During those visits, we did lots of sightseeing. We shopped at night markets. We ate at big banquets (no easy feat for a picky eater like me). We soaked at hot springs. And we met relatives to whom I wasn't sure *how* I was related. By the end, though, I had had an adventure and was always sad to say goodbye.

Something special to notice about this book:

In this story, I wanted to show the contrast between how Kylie feels at the beginning of her visit and at the end. You may have noticed the specific structure I used to highlight this change:

The first half of the story shows how Kylie feels uncertain about Amah and Taipei. It ends with Kylie considering an invitation from Amah to join her in the hot spring.

The second half begins when Kylie accepts Amah's invitation, and flows from there, with Kylie embracing Amah and Taipei with her whole heart.

From start to middle and middle to end, the lines are the same except in reverse order. But the surrounding context and punctuation changes allow them to have different meanings. Can you see how the lines from the first half of the story match to the lines from the second half of the story?

A NOTE FROM THE ILLUSTRATOR

I call my Taiwanese amah "waipo," which is the Mandarin name for my mother's mother. Before I was able to go with my mom to visit my waipo in Taiwan, she came to visit us in the States every few years. I remember the feeling of not being able to communicate well with her—she spoke the little English that she knew with me, and I was so shy to speak the little Chinese that I knew with her. Despite our timidity with language, we bonded over food.

I started visiting Taiwan yearly in college when my Mandarin was more fluent, and finally was able to live there for a year, studying and working as a designer. It was so wonderful to see my waipo so often and visit around Taiwan with my mother, aunt, and uncles. I even got to live in the middle of a night market—that meant delicious snacks, shopping, and performances every night! The places shown in this book are all special and have their own flavor. I hope this book will bring up some sweet memories, or inspire you to visit and learn more about Taiwan!

EXPLORE THE TAIPEI SIGHTS IN *AMAH FARAWAY*

Kylie learns to love Taipei like Amah does. It is so beautiful!

TAIPEI 101 once held the title of tallest building in the world (2004–2010). It has 101 floors above the ground and five floors below the ground. Its high-speed elevators zoom up to observation decks near the top of the building in thirty-seven seconds. Even cooler? It's built to survive typhoon-force winds and powerful earthquakes.

DA'AN FOREST PARK is to Taipei what Central Park is to New York City. Here, people escape into nature, away from the traffic and crowds of the big city. They have picnics. They stroll on paths. They listen to live music. They roller-skate at the skating rink. They visit the ecological pond that surrounds an island with hundreds of types of birds. They can even get their wiggles out at the playground.

NIGHT MARKETS are where crowds come to shop, play carnival games, and find sweet and savory snacks to eat. These street markets are open each day from late afternoon to late night. Two well-known night markets are Shilin and Raohe night markets. Shilin night market is the biggest and most popular with tourists. Raohe night market, also popular with tourists, is more family-friendly.

WULAI HOT SPRING is one of over one hundred hot springs in Taiwan. Hot springs are waters warmed by heat coming from inside the earth. The Taiwanese believe these waters, which are full of minerals, have healing powers. Wulai Hot Springs is located in beautiful Wulai, a mountain village first settled by the Atayal, one of the many indigenous peoples of Taiwan. It is an easy day trip away from Taipei.

Taiwanese Food

Instead of three meals, Taiwanese people famously have four—breakfast, lunch, dinner, and "midnight" snack. People wander night markets in search of late-night snacks that hit the spot. Pepper pork buns, oyster omelets, stinky tofu, fried chicken, and boba tea are some popular ones.

Besides being tasty, certain foods also have special meaning. This is especially clear at Lunar New Year. For example, the last dish served at a Chinese Lunar New Year banquet is a whole fish including head and tail. This symbolizes having plenty in the new year. Some fish is traditionally left over at the end of the meal to mean there will even be a surplus.

Other examples of dishes that have meaning:

Whole fish ⟶ Plenty
Whole chicken ⟶ Family togetherness
Uncut noodles ⟶ Long life
Turnip cakes ⟶ Luck
Dumplings ⟶ Good fortune
Pineapple ⟶ Good fortune

油條
yóu tiáo

豆漿
dòu jiāng

清蒸魚
qīng zhēng yú

雞湯
jī tāng

拖鞋
tuō xié

小籠包
xiǎo lóng bāo

公園
gōng yuán

蛋餅
dàn bǐng

國立中正
Guó lì zhōng zhèng
紀念堂
jì niàn táng

珍珠奶茶
zhēn zhū nǎi chá

機場
jī chǎng